A Trilogy OF LOVE

A

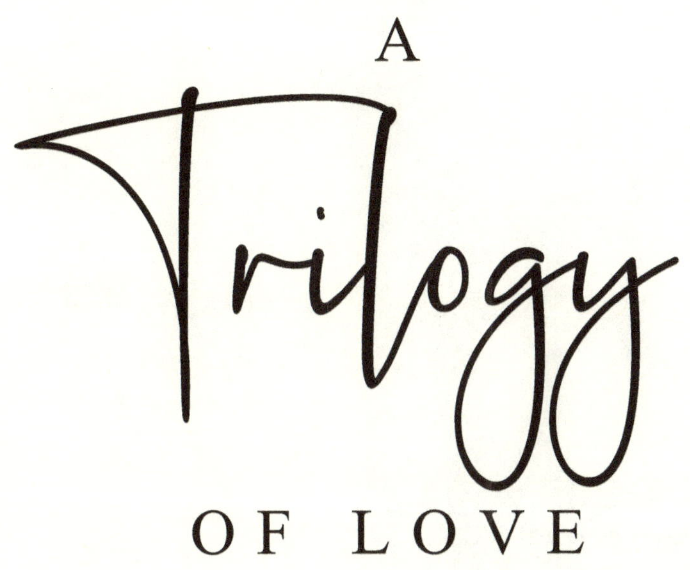

OF LOVE

G.B. MILLER

Contents

It Was the Right Thing

In previous years, Marty would be in his element at the Extravaganza. Wandering around the various vendors' booths to check the latest designs in jewelry, artwork and clothing; while also hitting the local food booths gorging himself silly on the fine local cuisine and all the while jamming to the hottest local bands. For all intents and purposes, he was the proverbial player of his town, and as such, he was doing his playing with his soulmate Jessie by his side.

However, this year things were devastatingly different. Exactly one week prior to the festival, Jessie had dropped the equivalent of Trump 1.0 on his tidy little world.

Marty had decided to surprise his lady love with lunch from her favorite grinder shop. So after picking up the one pound half grinder special, along with a half pint of slaw and a bottle of locally made ginger beer, he strolled over to her house with it. Upon arrival, he was about to open the front door when the sound of happy, albeit somewhat muffled, voices came drifting from the backyard.

Curious, he walked around the house towards the backyard and got the jaw-dropping surprise of his life: Jessie, in a lounge chair, topless, playing a mean game of tongue hockey with her bff Lisa.

Marty dropped her lunch on the patio deck. "What the fuck is going on here?!"

Startled, Jessie pushed Lisa off the chair and said, "It's not what you think!"

"Oh? It's not? If it isn't, then what is it exactly that you're doing with her?"

Jessie's silence confirmed Marty's original observation. He ripped off his pendant and threw it at her, where it bounced off her chest and landed in her lap, before squashing her lunch as he stormed off towards home.

Marty tried to get through the rest of the week the best he could, but failed miserably. Jessie was such an integral part of his life that no matter what he tried to do, he couldn't do it without her. By the time Saturday, the day of the festival, rolled around he was in such a deep dark hole of nothingness that he spent the entire morning in bed, shades down and the stereo blasting grindcore metal.

Doug was very worried about his best bud Marty. Being that they were all close friends since middle school, he was the one that more often than not picked up on all the subtle nuances and shade being thrown by the others. It just broke his heart to see Jessie play Marty for a fool.

Doug spent the entire week watching his friend slowly

spiral downwards into that dark hole of nothingness. After talking to Marty's mom and finding out just how bad Marty was, he decided to take action. Quickly realizing that this would be at the most a two man job, he decided to give a co-worker's friend who was a mutual friend of the former dynamic duo a call. Taking out his cell, he called his co-worker for her number, but the moment that he asked for it, he was put on hold.

After about a minute of dead silence, an irritated Doug was about to hang up. But before he could press the *end* button, the line suddenly crackled to life.

"Hello?" answered a young woman, who sounded way too caffeinated for a Saturday morning.

"Hi. Is this...Tamara?" asked Doug, who instantly had second thoughts about this phone call.

"Yes, it is. Who's this?"

"My name is Doug. We have a mutual friend in common, Jessie."

"Ex-friend in common."

"So...you heard, huh?"

"Yes."

Doug got the distinct impression that Tamara was just as bent about what Jessie had done as he was, if not more so. "I'm going over to rescue Marty from the dark dank hole that he stuck himself in, but I need a little help in doing so. Would you be able to meet me there and lend a hand if needed?"

Tamara thought about it for a moment or two. "Sure. I'll see you there in about ten minutes. Will that do?"

"That'll be fine. See you there."

Exactly ten minutes later, Doug was pulling into the drive-way when he saw a funky looking brunette step out of an even funkier looking mini Cooper and walk towards him. When he stepped out of his car, the funky looking brunette stuck out her hand.

"Tamara?" asked Doug as he cautiously shook her hand.

"Yes. Sorry about the appearance. I was just finishing up dress rehearsal when you'd called. I wanted to help, so I came right over."

"Rehearsal?"

"I play in a band."

"Cool."

"That's it? Just 'cool'?"

"Were you expecting something else?"

"Well...yeah. Most people give me the third degree when they meet me for the first time and find out I play in a band."

"So you play in a band and dress wickedly funky for it. I'm a photog that shoots exclusively for adult mags. If you think you got it bad, imagine the reactions I get when I tell people about my line of work."

"Good point." She fell silent for a moment, before remembering why she was there. "So, where do you want me to wait?"

"The porch. The hallway window is near the front on the second floor. If I need you, I'll just lean out and call you."

"Works for me," said Tamara as she sat on the porch rail and tried to get comfortable.

Doug tapped her leg before giving the front door a rap and walking into the house. He stopped in the living room to ex-change pleasantries with Marty's mom, before pointing his head towards the stairs. She nodded, so he ran up the stairs two at a time and was on the second floor in a matter of seconds. After pausing for a moment to catch his breath, he quietly walked to Marty's bedroom and knocked.

"Go away," said a voice tinged with sadness.

"I've come to take you away from this putrid cesspool that you made for yourself and insert you back amongst the living."

"Just leave me alone. Nothing bad can happen to me in my bed."

"I will not. What kind of friend would I be if I continued to leave you to your own devices?"

"A friend who knows when to leave well enough alone."

Doug raised an eyebrow, because he did leave well enough alone and shit hit the fan because of his inaction.

"I'm coming in and you will be leaving this house, either under your own power or not."

"Bullshit."

"No bullshit. What's it going to be? Under your own power or do I have to get mean?"

"Get mean."

Sighing, Doug walked out of the room and to the front hall window, where he promptly opened it and blew a short sharp whistle. Tamara stepped off the porch and spread out her arms, to which Doug sadly shook his head.

Tamara clapped her hands and walked inside. When she got to the living room, Marty's mother simply pointed towards the stairs.

"Thanks, and sorry for the intrusion."

"That's okay dear. Anyone who's a friend of Doug's is okay by me."

Blushing, she ran up the stairs and quickly found herself standing directly outside of Marty's room with Doug. He pulled out a pick and within a few seconds had the lock picked and the door open. On a count of 'three', he blasted through the door, grabbed Marty's legs and dragged him out of bed.

Tamara had grabbed the duffel bag that Doug had kicked over to her and threw it on Marty. Grabbing his arms, they hustled Marty out of the bedroom and to the staircase. Before they started down the stairs, she chucked the bag out of the window.

As they went through the living room, Doug said to Marty's mother, "We'll be at the Extravaganza for the rest of the day and I promise that he'll have a good time, even if it kills me. See you tonight."

Tamara added, "Thanks for having me, you have a lovely house."

Once they got to the front yard, they dropped Marty on the ground. Sticking a finger in his face, Doug said, "You can either get yourself dressed in private behind the shrubs, or Tamara and I will dress you right here in front of everyone. You got exactly ten seconds to decide."

"You're joking, right? You wouldn't dare do that to me in public, right?"

Marty saw Doug snatch the duffel bag and start to dig through it, so he said, "Holy cow, you're serious!"

He snatched the bag and sprinted towards the shrubs. Three minutes later he came out fully dressed, much to the relief of Doug and Tamara. Doug went to put his hand on Marty's shoulders, but he simply knocked it away and stormed out of the yard.

Doug sighed and said to Tamara, "I'm going to keep an eye on him. Will you be there later?"

"Absolutely. I'm performing tonight, but I'll make sure to bring a change of clothes for later. Whatever you do, do not let him see me perform. I want a chance to make a better first impression."

Puzzled, he asked, "What's the name of your band?"

"Paisley Pumpkin," before giving him a peck on the cheek and sprinting to her car.

Doug rubbed his cheek for a moment, smiled, then ran to catch up with Marty.

Doug could see that Marty was having an absolute miserable time at the Extravaganza. No matter what craft booth or food booth they'd hit, it was all met with the same sad indifference Marty had shown throughout the week.

"Dude, you're starting to bring me down to your level, and I don't want to come down to your level," said Doug as he took a seat in the gazebo for some relief from the afternoon heat.

"I'm sorry."

"Yeah, I know you are. Look, isn't there anything I can do to help you break out of this funk?"

Marty looked around for a little bit, then caught sight of a poster tacked up on the gazebo rail. "Hey, it looks like they got live music this year. Maybe that'll perk me up."

"Of course it will. Who's up next?"

Marty looked at his watch and said, "Some new local band called Paisley Pumpkin."

Doug spat out his drink.

Marty slapped his back and said, "Are you alright?"

Doug wiped his face and said, "I'm fine. I just swallowed wrong. Look, why don't we check out the beer garden. It's near the stage and you can listen to the music while sampling the various imports."

"But I want to see the band."

"And if we sit in the beer garden, it'll do wonders for my migraine."

Marty knew that Doug suffered from the occasional bad migraine. For the most part, he had them under control, but sometimes certain kinds of stress would cause them to reappear with a vengeance. "Okay, to the beer garden for my good friend. We can listen to the music while getting pleasantly hammered."

Sure enough, between the good beer and the rambling psycho-billy/alt country sound of Paisley Pumpkin, Marty was finally starting to loosen up. Gone was the tired sadness that had permeated his life for the past week, and in its place was the party hardy original that everyone had come to know and love for the past fifteen years.

By the time the band had finished its set some thirty minutes later, Marty was back to his old self. Doug, who had nursed his one beer for the entire set, was pleased about the way the day was turning out. As he was standing up to stretch and down the rest of his beer, someone had bumped into him. Turning around, the bumper was pointing at the stage.

Looking up, he saw that Tamara was waving at him and holding up a placard with a question mark on it. Doug held up his beer cup and she did a mini-fist pump, before running off the stage to wind down and change clothes.

Doug finished his beer and went off in search of Marty, who he'd found a few minutes later holding court at the far end of the beer garden. Clapping a hand on his shoulder, he said, "Time to get this show on the road. Got a lot more things to check out before the fireworks tonight."

Nodding in agreement, Marty bade everyone goodbye and followed Doug out of the beer garden and into the general public area. Before they even had a chance to clear the exit though, Doug and Tamara's hard work was dealt a heavy setback.

Jessie had walked by them with her new squeeze in tow.

Marty's good mood deflated faster than a souffle the second he'd seen Jessie walk by. He took a few steps towards her but Doug caught him by the belt and flung him in the opposite direction. Shaking his head, he glumly followed ast a safe distance and watched Marty stager from vendor to vendor and ride to ride without focus or need.

Doug began looking for Tamara throughout their wanderings, hoping that she was somewhere nearby to help salvage the rest of the day. More than once Marty caught him looking around and started to get annoyed with him for doing so.

Finally, after watching Doug do a complete three-sixty for the third time in less than three minutes, he detonated.

"Who the hell are you looking for? Are you trying to find that super dyke and her skanky girlfriend so that you can rub it into my face for being such a loser?!"

"It's nothing like that. I'm looking for a friend who promised to meet up with us once she got off work."

"Yeah, right. A friend. That's rich. You know what, I am out of here. I'll talk to you later, maybe. And by the way, thanks for nothing."

Marty turned to go home but immediately slammed into someone and sent them and himself sprawling to the ground. Doug helped him up, before they both helped the young lady up and brushed off the dirt and grass. Marty took a couple of feeble swipes before dropping to his knees sobbing.

Doug leaned in and spoke to Tamara. "Glad you showed. He's a mess again because he saw Jessie walk by the beer garden with her new squeeze. I'm going to head towards the other end of the park. Good luck and be gentle with him."

She squeezed his arm and said, "Thanks, and I will."

Tamara knelt down in front of Marty and gently cupped his chin. Raising his head, she wiped his eyes dry and said, "Hey, there's no need for tuning on the water faucet. See? No lasting damage done, save for a sore butt and a tweaked ego."

"It's not you. I...I got dumped earlier in the week," he said between heaves.

She placed a finger on his lips and said, "Why don't we move this conversation to that bench next to the fence? As it is, we're just in the way and over there, we won't be and will have a little privacy to boot. What do you say?"

Marty stifled his sobs and nodded, so Tamara took his hand and brought him over to the ebench. Sitting down, she said, "I'm going to get something to eat. Do you want anything?"

Calming down a little, he said, "A pretzel would be nice."

"A pretzel it is. I'll be back in a few."

Tamara walked towards one of the food booths and along the way spotted Doug leaning against a rail. Picking up a small rock, she threw a high arcing shot that nailed him on the head.

Startled, he rubbed his head and looked around for the person that threw it. Several seconds later he spotted Tamara waving at him. He started picking his way through the growing crowd and soon met her in a line at one of the good booths.

"So?" asked Doug.

"About fifty-fifty."

He gave her a ten and said, "Tomorrow."

"Tomorrow?"

"Tomorrow. I'm heading for home."

"You're leaving me alone with him?"

"Any reason why I shouldn't?"

Before she could answer, he gave her a peck on the cheek, then slipped out of the line and headed for home.

A few minutes later, Tamara had bought two pretzels and two sodas, and was soon heading back to where she'd left Marty. Along the way, she thought about what she wanted to say, because quite frankly, she was in love with Marty. Ever since Jessie had showed her his picture several months ago, she wanted to possess him. Now that he was so tantalizingly closer, she started to second guess herself.

What if I misread his signals and say the wrong thing? Or worse, do something wrong? What if he takes what I say the wrong way and tells me to shove off?

Marty had spotted Tamara walking back from the food booth, and after staring at her for a spell, suddenly remembered where he'd seen her before. "Before" was at the house, dressed in a funky outfit, wearing a bizarro hairdo and looking like an escapee from a psych ward. "Now", she was looking quite beautiful and very sensuous.

She was wearing a tasteful grass-colored summer dress, her long auburn hair, which meshed quite nicely with her tan, was now hanging loose about her shoulders and back, and completely the ensemble was a matching pair of leather sandals. She had a bounce to her step that made her hair trail like blown dandelions and her curves were tastefully accentuated when the breeze caught her dress just right.

When Tamara arrived at the bench, she handed Marty his pretzel and soda, before taking a seat next to him. They sat there in silence, each leisurely consuming their food and drink while thinking about how the day was treating them.

As the warm afternoon gradually faded away and the cool evening began to take shape, Tamara decided to make her move. Throwing her empty soda cup away, she asked, "I'm going for a walk around the pond. Would you like to join me?"

Marty finished his pretzel and took a long last swig of his soda, before answering in a tone that gave Tamara a sliver of hope. "Sure. Be more than happy to join you."

She stood up and before long was weaving her way through the festival crowd. Marty tried to follow but lost her the moment she dipped a shoulder and squeezed between two rather large ladies. After pausing for a few seconds to think, he took off in the direction of where he thought she might have gone.

While zigzagging through the crowd, his foot caught the edge of the pond walkway. Quickly losing his balance, he stumbled for several steps before landing face first in the tall grass on the other side.

Tamara saw the entire incident unfold in front of her, so after stepping to her right, looked down and said, "Great save."

Marty turned over and said, "Thanks, care to give me a hand?"

She clapped sarcastically and said, "How's that?"

"Fun*ny*."

She bent down and sasid, "Sorry. Force of habit. Here, give me your hand."

After getting him up, she began bruising off the dirt and grass. Reading his facial expression, she said, "Both. I don't like being in crowds much and sometimes my humor can be off putting."

"Really? I wouldn't have known if you hadn't told me."

Tamara went wide-eyed for a moment before falling silent. She finished brushing him off, kissed his cheek and said, "I should leave. It was very nice to have met you. Tell Doug that I tried my best but it just didn't click between us."

Marty thought long and hard about what she had said as he watched her walk towards the gazebo. Suddenly, a light bulb blew in his tiny little brain, and he ran after her. Within a minute he had caught up with Tamara and grabbed her arm. She spun around and punched him hard in the stomach.

Marty doubled over, dropped to his knees and once again face planted and ate grass. It took Tamara a few seconds to figure who she had hit, but when she did, she dropped to her knees and cradled his head in her lap.

Crying as she stroked his head, she said, "I am so sorry for hitting you. I thought someone was attacking me so I threw a hard one the second I was turned around."

Marty waited for the pain to subside, before slowly rolling on his back. Grimacing as he sat up, he said, "You know, I think you bruised a rib with that punch, but that's not what I want to talk to you about. I want to talk about the fact that we make an interesting non-couple."

"Non-couple? What's a non-couple?" she asked while drying her eyes with her hair.

"Us."

"Us?"

"Yes, us. As in, me having a crappy day because my steady girlfriend dumped me for another woman. As in, you trying to hit on me and doing it all wrong by actually hitting me. So how 'bout we try being a couple for a change?"

"And how do you propose to do that?"

"Watch, and be amazed when you finally get the drift of my little one act play and start having fun."

Marty stood up and helped Tamara to her feet. He then took a napkin out of his pocket and cleaned her face, before walking her to the gazebo and sitting her down on the bench. After making a few gestures on how he wanted her to sit, he beeped her nose, walked down the steps and stopped some five feet away.

He turned around, and after taking a deep breath to kill the butterflies, walked up the stairs and stopped in front of her.

Clearing his throat, he said, "Excuse me, but I happened to be walking by just now and I saw that you were sitting there all by your lonesome. Are you in fact, sitting all by your lonesome?"

"I am."

"And might you be waiting for someone?"

She smiled shyly and said, "Perhaps."

"Well then, may I sit here and keep you company until that particular someone happens to come by?"

"You may."

"Thanks. By the way, my name is Marty. To whom do I have the pleasure of not only talking to on this gorgeous Saturday evening, but sitting next to as well?"

"Tamara."

"Tamara. What a lovely name. Would happen to be that same Tamara who sang here tonight with the band Paisley Pumpkin? And helped my good friend Doug carry me out of my house and forced me to go to this festival, for which I might add, I am very grateful for."

Blushing, she said, "I am."

"Well then," said Marty as he stood up. "Would you be interested in taking a stroll around this lovely pond with a guy who sometimes needs to be told point blank what someone is trying to say to him?"

Tamara held out her hand and said very quietly, "Yes, I would be interested in taking a stroll around this lovely pond with a guy who sometimes needs to be told point blank about what someone is trying to say. So long as the guy doesn't mind walking with a gal who isn't used to dealing with the opposite sex on a personal level.

He took her hand and said, "Not one bit."

They exited the gazebo and began their stroll around the pond. A few minutes into their walk, they came across a family of ducks that were bathing and relaxing. He saw her walk to the edge of the pond, take out a piece of pretzel and kneel down in the grass.

Several seconds later, he watched in quiet amazement as the family of ducks approached her, quacked a couple of times, before taking a pretzel piece out of her outstretched hand.

After watching the entire family take their pretzel piece and waddle away, Marty quietly tapped her shoulder. After waiting a few seconds, he knelt down and said, "You seem to have a peculiar connection with the feathered friends."

She leaned in and said, "It's a gift. Somehow, they can sense my emotional state and act accordingly. A bit freaky, but it certainly does restore my inner chi afterwards."

He waited until the last duck finished eating before standing up. Holding out his hand, he asked, "Ready to continue?"

Wiping her hand on the grass, she took his and suddenly had a tingly feeling come over her. Looking up, she saw that Marty's eyes were a deep hazel that sparkled with an intensity that she'd never seen in anyone else before, and for a brief moment, a small wave of fear suddenly gripped her.

But just as quick, the wave was batted away by his reassuring smile, which soothed her spirit as well.

They continued their walk, making small talk and commenting on the sights and sounds of the pond. To the casual observer it appeared that nothing of note was happening, the fact of the matter was quite pleasantly the opposite.

Marty and Tamara never broke hand contact, so while they were walking, they were also playing an intricate game of handsies. Not only was that game being expertly played but they were also connecting on an emotional level too. By the time they arrived back at the gazebo, they were talking exclusively through finger touches and hand squeezes.

Marty took out his phone to check the time and said, "Babe, it's almost nine. What time did they say the fireworks would be launched?"

He called me babe! "Nine-thirty."

"Perfect. I have just the spot for us to watch the show."

He led her to a small secluded spot near the waterfalls, where they could watch the fireworks in private. It was located in a small grove of trees, with a blanket set up in the middle and two pairs of headphones hanging off a nearby branch.

He first got her situated on the blanket before making himself comfortable and handing her a pair of headphones. She took them, then threw him a questioning look.

"It gets quite loud over here, as we're about fifty yards away from the launch site. This is my traditional viewing spot for the fireworks and I want to share them with someone special. So if you would, please put on the headphones as the show will be starting in a few minutes.

Tamara put on the headphones and waited for the fireworks to start. While waiting, she thought about how much she was out of her element with Marty. She decided to tell him that in spite of what went on today, it really wasn't going to work out, when his hand gently touched her waist. With that one gesture, her resolve melted away and she snuggled up to him.

Cupping his face, she gazed deeply into his eyes, smiled and delivered a deep passionate kiss. In that very instant, all of the fireworks were launched.

A Singular Couple

I finished the last of my coffee and took a seat in a small cubbyhole at my local library. After spending a few minutes waiting for my wonky laptop to become the piece of electronic deviltry that perpetually infuriates me, I quickly began pounding away on my keyboard.

That lasted for a good three minutes as the words poured out of me so fast that I had to actually yell at myself to slow down. So you can imagine my surprise when I took a short breather to see where I was, and found that I wasn't anywhere. All of my furious typing amounted to nothing as my screen was completely blank.

Swearing loudly, I was about to toss my laptop like a frisbee when I stupidly realized that the reason why nothing was on my screen, was that nothing was on my screen. In my haste to start my story, I had forgotten one key component to my story: Word.

Banging my head on the desk, I quickly opened up Word and several seconds later, the words were pouring out like a swollen waterfall. This fantastic deluge caused me to block out my surroundings, thus not realizing that my good friend was standing next to me until she had delivered a hard slap to my freshly shaven head.

"What the hell?!" I yelled before turning around.

"You wrote something offensive."

"What?"

"You heard me," she repeated as she raised her hand again.

Flinching, I said, "Yeah, I heard you, but can you give me some specifics as to what the offensive story might be? Simply saying that I wrote something offensive is akin to me saying that I like your cooking."

She threw the story in question in my face and said, "This."

I look at the story. "Dirty Knees. Good story. Problem is…?"

"Sex."

I briefly scan the first page. "What sex?"

"What do you mean, 'what sex'? The entire story is dripping with it. As a matter of fact, all of your stories are dripping with sex!"

"Excuse you? Did you even read it to the end? There is no blatant sex. It's all suggestive."

"It still makes me uncomfortable."

Clearly, I had struck a nerve. I was curious not only about what the nerve was, but how I had struck it to begin with. "And I make you uncomfortable, how?"

She pulls up a chair and sits. Shifting uncomfortably, she eventually leans in and whispers, "Because it comes from you."

"What?"

"Keep your voice down! Do you want people to know your business?"

I closed my laptop and said, "What does that got to do with our current conversation?"

"Well...knowing you like I do, all this talk about sex makes me uncomfortable."

"Sex sells. No sex, hint or otherwise, makes my stories wickedly dull, and I simply do not write dull stories."

"I didn't say that."

"No, no you didn't. You said," and I whispered this last part. "I make you feel uncomfortable."

Turning red, she stood up and snatched the story from hands. Rolling it up, she shoved it back into her jeans and stormed out of the reference area.

Rubbing my eyes, I briefly thought about the absurdity of the situation, before reopening my laptop and returning to my story. Within a minute, the swollen waterfall had returned and my friend was but a distant memory.

Or so I thought. She soon reappeared and the general public got a rare glimpse of how she was when someone had the temerity to tick her off.

She slapped my head to get my attention again, which in turn caused me to turn around. This time, instead of face-timing her, I got face-time with a bucket of ice water and two towels.

Pursuing my lips, I said, "Let me put my laptop away."

She waited until I was done, then asked, "Done?"

I first looked at her, then at the bucket. "Done."

"Stand up."

I stood up and stepped away from the table. She unbuttoned my jeans, then poured the entire contents of the bucket into my jeans. When she'd finished, she handed me the towels, buttoned my jeans and sat me down.

"Anything else?" I asked, fervently hoping that no more abuse would be inflicted on my person.

She leaned in so that prying ears couldn't hear. "Your big sister says that the next time you want to show me your writing, don't."

She tapped my cheek a couple of times, before turning on her heel and walking away, leaving me alone with my laptop, my wet jeans and a thoroughly chilled imagination.

About a week later, I was sitting in the park watching a tai chi class. I certainly wasn't watching it for the view, but for an article that I was going to write for a small suburban monthly.

Scribbling away in my notebook, I was so engrossed in what I was doing that I didn't hear her approach. My train of thought was interrupted when I felt a very heavy weight on my shoulder and saw a large shadow on my notebook. When I looked up, a pair of smiling light brown eyes and corresponding complexion was staring back at me. I quickly slid off the bench, scrambled to my feet and ran towards the walkway.

"Why are you over there?" she asked innocently.

Snorting, I said, "Because I remembered what you did the last time I wrote something that you didn't like, and I don't want a repeat performance."

"Look, we're outdoors and I'm unarmed."

I gave her the once over, and taking into consideration the snug jeans and loose t-shirt, I said, "Not quite."

Blushing, it took her a moment to regain her composure. In the meantime I made a big production out of making a large check mark, before flashing a dopey grin.

She returned the smile, before getting serious. "I didn't come here to inflict any more humiliation on you, if that's what you're worried about."

"Perhaps."

Sighing, she said, "Please come back to the bench and I promise not to do anything rash."

I could see that she was agitated about something, so in spite of what went down at the library, I went back to the bench and sat down. The second my ass touched wood, she moved over, which caused me to quickly plant my ass on the grass. She slid further down to where I was, brought her legs up and waited for me to settle down.

Seemingly satisfied that I was going to stay put, she took out a fattie and lit it. She took a couple hard drags, before offering me a hit, of which I politely declined.

Shrugging, she spent the next few minutes becoming progressively stoned. I had heard stories about her ginormous consumption of cannabis, but I'd never personally witnessed it.

Until now.

Crawling over to her so that we could continue our conversation with a modicum of privacy, I sat down in front of her and tapped her knee to get her attention.

She looked down and for a moment, seemed genuinely puzzled. But it quickly passed and she asked, "What?"

"You tell me. You're the one who interrupted my work assignment, not me."

"Right."

She stubbed out her fattie and stuck it behind her ear. Clearing her throat, she took a deep breath and fell silent as the cannabis wormed its way through her nervous system.

I waited to see if she was going to come out her Mary Jane haze before deciding to take the nuclear option that would bring her back to the present.

I knew what I wanted to do. In fact, if I did it, it would have a profound impact on our friendship. So I took my time and went over all the possible outcomes should I go nuclear. I covered all the angles, checked all my escape routes, but most importantly, I checked to make sure that my sneakers were tied.

I stood up and began flexing my legs while periodically stealing a look at my friend to see if she was back. If she was, there would be no need for me to go nuclear and complicate our friendship.

Her glazed look confirmed the plan of attack that I needed to pursue. I steeled my nerve and slowly walked back to the bench and leaned in. I brushed a few hair strands from her face in preparation to do what I really didn't want to do.

I knew it was the right thing to do, but it didn't make it any easier for me knowing that it was the right thing to do. Yet, I hesitated. Why? Maybe it was that I still respected her both as a person and as a beautiful woman, who even at her late age can still make heads turn.

As I was debating myself, a friend of mine happened to walk by. He saw my confused expression, so he decided to stop by and investigate.

"Dude! What is up my man?"

"Oh, hi...umm...Jon."

"Wow, you sound so excited to see me," said Jon as he looked at the stoner on the bench. "Who's the zombie?"

"Michelle," I said absentmindedly. Suddenly a light bulb blew. I grabbed his arm and dragged him over to the bench.

"Jon!" I exclaimed as I just about tore his arm off while shaking his hand. "Am I ever glad to see you! Say, are you still unattached?"

"Yeah. Why?" he answered warily.

"I need a favor. I need to get my friend back to here."

"So?"

"So...there's only one way that I know of that will do the trick."

Jon went wide-eyed and said, "Not on your life, buddy boy. You are on your own with this one."

"But---"

"No 'buts' about it. I know her, and trust me, I do not want to ever get on her bad side. I like living in one piece, and if I do what you're suggesting, I won't be in one piece. I'll be in multiple little pieces. People will talk about me in the past tense and I'm too young to be talked about in the past tense."

"Alright already. I don't need to hear any more whining. I get the point. I'll talk to you later."

Jon clapped me on the shoulder and said, "I doubt it."

I watched him leave and sadly realized that if I wanted

someone to do what I'd suggested to Jon, that someone would have to be me. Resigned to my fate, I sat down next to her and once again brushed a few hair strands from her face. Gently cupping her face, I stared deep into those thoughtful light brown eyes, and kissed her.

The initial response from her when I'd finished was a devilish grin appeared on her face, so I repeated the effort with a little more passion behind it. This time, I got the response that I really didn't want. She grabbed my face, pulled me in and delivered a passionate kiss of her own. Before I could respond, I found myself in a beautiful woman's warm embrace and doing something that I haven't done since I was a teenager.

After a few minutes of passionate tongue hockey, we disconnected and she caressed my cheek. Suddenly something clicked in her head and she went wide-eyed in shock. She shoved me off the bench, which made me somersault and land flat on my face.

She quickly followed up by pouncing on me like a tiger making a kill. She turned me over, sat on my chest and pinned my shoulders with her knees.

We stared at each other for a good solid minute, as neither of us wanted to give the other the satisfaction that a major faux pas was performed. She sat there with arms crossed and throwing off the kind of vibe that told me that I was in some very deep shit.

Me? I certainly wasn't going anywhere. The few attempts made at getting up were met by her plump body bouncing on my stomach, and the one time I tried to speak, I received a right cross and a black eye for my efforts.

Giving me a black eye seemed to quiet her rage a little. She readjusted her position so that she was on my hips instead, and her feet were digging into my armpits as opposed to knees on shoulders. Plus, she now seemed to be receptive to having a normal conversation. Sighing hard, I thought about what I wanted to say, steeled what little spine I had left, and plowed forward.

"I gather you're a little angry over what'd just happened."

"Damn straight. What the hell possessed you to do that?"

"I needed you."

"Excuse me?! You needed me?!"

Seeing how those three words amped up her anger again as she raised a fist, I said, "Let me rephrase that."

"You better."

"I needed you back here."

"Excuse me?"

"Here. You know, the now. The present. Today."

"I get the point."

She grew silent as she thought about accepting my explanation. In the meantime, I thought about what I'd done and hoped to God that I could somehow salvage our friendship. I also kept my eyes closed, since the way she was sitting was lending itself to a provocative 'show and tell'.

Suddenly I felt a sharp pain in my knees. I opened my eyes and saw to my annoyance that Michelle had readjusted her position and was now sitting cross-legged on my knees and hips.

"What the fuck?"

"I'm trying to get comfortable."

"Well, I'm going numb from the excess baggage. Get comfy on the ground."

"Are you calling me fat?"

Without even engaging my brain, I said, "Plump."

She slowly rolled off, making sure that my knees got bent the other way, then stood up and walked over to the bench. 'Course, she did take a minor shortcut to get there via my stomach, which made me curl up to wait for the pain to subside.

She sat down on the bench and took out her fattie. After lighting it, she took deep thoughtful tokes while waiting for me to recover from her latest assault on my junk. The pain eventually subsided, but since my legs were numb, I rolled over to the bench. I slowly sat up and grabbed the fattie from her mouth.

I took a sniff and quickly stubbed it out. "This is what got us into our current predicament."

Not receiving any response, I immediately thought the worst, and waving my hand simply confirmed it.

Once again, my friend Jon happened to be walking by. He took one look and said, "Isn't this where I had left you about a half hour ago?"

"Things did go bump while you were gone."

"Anything I can do?"

I looked at her for a moment, before remembering an old paint bucket in the trunk of my car. "Jon, can you get something from my car for me? You know what I drive, right?"

"Sure do. What do you need?"

"A bucket. You'll find it in the trunk," I said tossing him the keys.

He caught them and said, "Back in a couple of tics."

A couple of tics later, Jon returned with the bucket. He handed it and the keys to me and asked, "What are you going to do with the bucket?"

I didn't answer, but simply raised a finger to my lips.

Curious, he watched as I walked over to the pond and dipped the bucket into it. About thirty seconds later, the bucket was filled with icy cold pond water, pond lilies, bullfrogs and a thin layer of pond scum.

Again putting a finger to my lips, I walked over to Michelle and sat down next to her. Placing the bucket next to me, I tried one last time to bring her back to the present. Failing again, I grabbed the bucket, stood up and walked behind her. Flashing Jon a dopey grin, I then proceeded to empty the contents of the buck over her.

A look of total shock appeared on her face after I'd emptied the bucket all over her. I gave the bucket to Jon, clapped my hands and took a pond lily from her head and handed it to her.

Jon must've seen something that I, being in the middle of my happy dance, didn't see. He yelled, "He did it!" before flinging the bucket and running away from us and out of the park.

I waved goodbye and turned my attention back to Michelle. Spying a large bump that was moving across her chest, I stuck my hand under her shirt and pulled out a rather fat bullfrog. I dried it on my jeans, dropped it in her lap and said "Here's a friend of yours."

I stepped away and turned my back to her so that I could light up a cigarette without the wind blowing out the flame. I got it lit and as I turned around to take a puff, I saw her take the pond lily that I had given to her and place it gently on the bench. She then grabbed the bullfrog and another pond lily from under her shirt and created a frog sandwich. Flashing me an evil smile, she squashed the bullfrog like a hamburger patty.

I spat out my cigarette and took off running.

I ran like a man being chased by an irate Doberman. I had gotten such a fantastic jump that by the time Michelle took off after me, I was through the exit near the baseball field a quarter mile away. I briefly stopped to catch my breath, but when I heard her yell, "Motherfucker! I'm gonna pound your brains into hamburger!" I took off again, this time down the middle of the street.

Dodging cars, I was momentarily able to once again put a fair distance between myself and the hound from hell. I should mention that even though I was running at a fast clip, Michelle, who did long distance running as a hobby, was moving at a steady lope and within a few minutes had closed the gap.

Once she'd gotten within earshot again, she threw out another threat. "Listen motherfucker! You better stop running and take your punishment like the man you're pretending to be! If you don't, then when I do catch you, I'll inflict double the pain just because I had to chase your skinny white ass all over this fuckin' town!"

I responded the only way that was left to me. I slammed on the brakes and ran towards her, with the intention of bowling her over and delaying her just long enough for me to get to my car and leave. Accelerating, I got close enough to launch a flying tackle, which neither connected nor surprised her. Instead, she caught me in the air, spun and drove me two inches into the ground with a heavy power slam.

While I was writing around in pain from a couple of cracked ribs, she sat down next to me and spent the next few minutes throwing dirty looks. When I'd tried to see what she was going, she grabbed my head and shoved me back down.

After a while she made a decision on what she wanted to do next. She crawled over and sat cross-legged on my waist and stomach. She then asked, "Are you ready?"

Swallowing hard, I said through clenched teeth, "Do I have a choice?

She took out a fattie and searched my pockets for a light. Naturally I flinched while she was searching, so naturally she reached behind and punched me where it would hurt the most.

"Fuck!" I yelled.

"Hardly."

Hardly?"

She lit the fattie, took a heavy drag and smiled.

After taking that king sized hit, Michelle spent the next few minutes letting the bitter taste numb her body and tranquilize her mind. Outwardly, the only sign that the cannabis was having any effect was a tight smile and a languid stare at the smoldering fattie nestled between her fingers. Inwardly, she was a high speed train approaching a sharp bend, as the thought of what she wanted to do next paralyzed her with fear.

Then in a mental blink of a brain cell, she obliterated that fear and made her decision. Flicking away the fattie, she readjusted her position by straddling my chest. Looking up, I couldn't help notice the diamond stud in her belly button and the tattoo that surrounded it.

She'd noticed the subtle change in my eyes and asked in a quiet voice, "Would you like to have a closer look?"

"I don't know. You're not gonna put another hurt on me if I say yes, are you? I asked worriedly. I was still in a bit of pain from the cracked ribs and the last thing that I wanted was those ribs to be the easiest thing to recover from.

She leaned forward and cupped my chin."No, I won't."

I saw those light brown eyes shine with a genuine warmth that scared me. Nevertheless, I steeled my nerve and said, "Then yes, I would like to have a closer look."

She looked to see if anyone was around, but considering my resting place was a grove of trees, we were pretty much safe from prying eyes. She carefully rolled up her t-shirt until her entire stomach was exposed.

"You can touch it if you want. I made you a promise and I'm sticking to it."

I saw upon closer examination that she had a rather large diamond stud in her belly button and judging from where the tattoo was situated, it acted like a bejeweled eye. The tattoo itself was an intricately designed butterfly, as the antennae and wings started at the halfway point of her stomach and continued downwards until it disappeared below her waistline. The wings were filled with electric colors and detail, and the wings moved hypnotically as she breathed. She shivered a little as I traced the outline of the butterfly with my finger and the vibes that she was throwing told me that stopping would be a wise course of action.

I say 'shivering' because even though I was getting a few sensual facial responses, her body language was saying in no uncertain terms that to continue would be detrimental to my well being. So I lowered her shirt and gently patted her stomach.

"Now, there has to be something else going on in your world besides this hot tat and wicked diamond stud piercing, because there's no way in hell you would have gotten stoned, which forced me to do something that I didn't want to do, which caused you to not only beat the snot out of me, but give me an intimate peek at your body as well. So please, tell me what the hell do you really want?"

She smoothed out her shirt and sighed heavily before speaking. "What I really want is to discuss a personal problem and I was embarrassed to talk to you about it."

"So getting stoned was your way of talking about it?"

"Well….yeah. Getting stoned was the only way that I knew of to talk to you about it."

"Come again?"

"I should clarify, shouldn't I?"

"That would be a good idea. But first, could you get off my chest? The added weight of you to my cracked ribs is making it difficult to breath."

Pursing her lips, she rolled onto the grass and stretched out her legs. I instantly grabbed my stomach and rolled over. I don't know how long I stayed like that, but eventually I felt someone tapping my head, and since the pain had dropped to a dull ache, I rolled back over.

Opening my eyes, I quickly realized that I was lying in between a pair of well toned yet very soft legs. Looking up, I found myself staring in Michelle's smiling face. I thought about sitting up, but she just gently shook her head and squashed that thought.

"Well, this is a pleasant surprise," I said as I rested my arms on her thighs.

"Yeah, I thought you'd find this more to your liking than I was sitting on your chest.

She fell silent as what she wanted to tell me her problem was beginning to weigh heavily on her, so I tried to put her at ease.

"Look, whatever it is that you need to say, just say it. I won't get upset and I won't be offended. You had a reason to talk to me to begin with, otherwise---". I didn't get a chance to finish because she finally blurted out the reason for being at the park today.

"I think you're becoming more than just a friend to me."

More than a friend? "How so?"

"For starters, do you think that I would let just any man touch me like you did a few moments ago?"

Not in my lifetime. "No, I suppose not."

"Of course not. Furthermore , I have never gone to greater lengths in order to find someone on a weekday morning, like I did with you. And---"

"There's an 'and'?"

By this point, she had found her confidence again and was back to her old mercurial self, which usually meant that I would have to tough out this disjointed conversation until she arrived at whatever weird conclusion she was driving to.

"Yes, there is. We bicker like a married couple. We make up almost like a married couple. Shit, we even do things to each other that only married couples do."

But we ain't married. Shit, we ain't even dating each other. Shit, is she suggesting…? "So my trusted compadre, if I'm not just a friend, then what am I?"

I really needed to bring this to a head, because as much as I respected her as a close friend, the last thing I wanted to do was to take this friendship down a road that could eventually destroy us.

She was about to answer, when she suddenly held up a finger. She then untied her ponytail and shook her hair loose. When she'd finished, it had cascaded down her back and over her face until it had created a soft sensual veil. Leaning forward, she lightly touched and teased my face with it, which in short order drove me mad with desire.

Damn! She is suggesting that! "Stop that," I said as I slid a little further down on the grass.

"Don't you like that?"

I looked into her eyes and saw that she was beaming with happiness. I didn't want to destroy what she'd found but I really needed to put things back to the way they were. "I do, but I don't."

She straightened up and drew her legs until she was sitting cross-legged. Crestfallen, she said, "I just made a fool out of myself, didn't I?"

I rolled over and sat up. I saw the pained look and watery eyes, and for the first time today, I felt genuinely ashamed about what I did earlier. I crawled over until I was face to face, then gently cupped her chin, brushed her hair back and dried her eyes.

"You could never do that. It took a lot of courage for you to say and do what you were doing, and I say that because I know how you really cherish your privacy. Don't you think for one moment that I didn't appreciate the offer, because while the offer was real, I just couldn't accept and return it the same way. You know I do love you, but only as the sister I never had, not as a potential girlfriend."

"Only as a sister? Not even as a friend with benefits?" she cried.

Again, wiping away her tears, I quietly caressed her cheek while I thought about what to say next. Apparently, I had her teetering on the edge and I really didn't want her to fall into the abyss. Kissing her forehead, I said, "You already provide a special kind of friendship, one that comes with partial benefits."

I saw that breathing had steadied and the hard lines on her face soften, so taking that as a positive sign, I plowed on.

"I enjoy the partial benefits that you give to me and I would hope that those same partials that I give to you, you enjoy as well."

She flipped her hair and tentatively nodded in agreement.

"I'm glad. Since we're in agreement about the partials we give to each other, why ruin it by trying to take our friendship to the next level? I'll always be here for you, whenever you need advice, to vent or to simply shoot the breeze. Nothing can ever change what we have going on together."

She exhaled softly before grabbing me in a very warm embrace. She then whispered, "I truly appreciate what you'd just said. I just want to let you know that not only do I forgive you what you did earlier, but I do love you the same way that you love me."

She paused for a moment as she suddenly shoved me hard to the ground and quickly sat on my back. Leaning in, she again whispered, "If you tell anyone, and I mean anyone, what actually happened here today, I will break all four of your limbs and take permanent possession of that tiny little piece of meat dangling between your legs. Do I make myself clear?"

I turned my head sideways and said, "Crystal clear. I'm glad we were able to reach a mutual understanding."

"Word. Anyways, you take care of yourself. I wouldn't want anyone else to fuck you up, because I want that pleasure all for my very own."

Rolling off, she then gave my manhood a hard squeez, before giving the top of my sunburned head the briefest of kisses. Then like a pleasant nightmare, she was gone, while I sat there trying to figure out how, in the span of one week, I had gained a wife.

Friends With Benefits

Julee had just gotten herself situated on the couch for a dull early morning of game play when the main entrance buzzer went off. Sighing, she paused her game and walked over to the intercom. Wiping her hand on her jeans, she pressed the 'talk' button.

"Who be there bothering me?"

"Bobbi."

"Bobbi?"

"Yes."

Julee looked at the wall clock and said, "It's two a.m. What the hell are you doing here?"

"I needed to talk to my bestie, so can I come in?"

Sighing for a moment, she said, "Sure."

Julee pressed another button and a few minutes later heard a knock on her door. After straightening out her clothes and finger combing her curls, she opened the door. There, standing in front of her and looking totally crushed, was her bestie Bobbi.

"What's wrong?"

"I got into another argument with Julias. Can I come in?"

"Sure thing," said Julee as she opened the door to let her in. Bobbi gave her a peck on the cheek then walked directly into the living room and plopped down on the couch.

Julee exhaled sharply, before closing the door and waking into the kitchen. She rummaged around in the fridge for several seconds, before pulling out two long neck stouts and some fatties.

Handing one of each to Bobbi, she sat down in the lounge chair, popped hers open and lit her fattie. After taking a large drag and a deep swig from hers, she asked, "So what did you two fight about this time?"

Bobbi took a long swig hers and swung her legs onto the couch. She quickly lit her fattie, took a couple of tokes and then fell silent.

Julee got up and walked over to the couch. Taking up a spot directly behind her, she knelt down and began to tenderly massage her neck and shoulders while taking the occasional ear nibble.

For the longest time, Bobbi remained lost in thought, which was due to the fact that she didn't know how to tell Julee that her latest blowout with Julias was about their friendship. She began to purr softly as Julee's massage was driving her mad with desire.

"Bobbi, what was the fight about this time?" she asked again, this time in a sultry voice that made Bobbi drop a gear with her purring.

For the past twenty years, Bobbi and Julee were about as close to one another as two people could possibly get without being lovers or spouses. Theirs was a friendship that had no boundaries and quite often it took precedence over whatever nominal relationships they had going on at the time.

Even after performing her signature massage, Julee could still feel the nervous energy pouring out from Bobbi. Kneeling down, she whispered, "It was about me, wasn't it?"

Bobbi took another long swig of her stout and said, "Yah, it was."

"Why on earth did you tell him about us?"

"He's into that whole honesty bullshit, so I thought---"

"So you thought that telling him about your friendship with me would be a good thing?"

"Well….yah."

Julee kissed her cheek, before getting up. She walked around to the front of the couch and sat down. She carefully pulled off her pj top, tossed it to the side and leaned back.

"So my bestie, what can I do to put you back into the proper frame of mind so that you can repair your relationship with Julias?"

"I don't know. I really want to make this relationship with Julias work, but he's such a deep freeze ice king that I get exhausted from the effort of trying to break through."

"Does him being an ice king make him jealous about me and insecure about himself?"

Bobbi down the last of her stout and said, "Pretty much."

"And you need what from me?" asked Julee as she moved over to Bobbi's lap.

"Understanding."

"That goes without saying."

"True," said Bobbi, who just noticed that Julee was sitting on her lap making googly eyes.

Smiling sadly, she said, "Listen, I think it's high time that we looked at taking care of your needs tonight for a change. So my little ninja warrior, I heard through the sake-vine that your new boy toy has been putting you into a world of a destroyed libido lately. Is that true?"

A sad smile coupled with a repressed sob told Bobbi that tonight was going to be more about comforting an old friend than her doing the sensually nasty.

"So what kind of is the serious pain to your libido is he inflicting on you?"

Julee leaned back and sadly ran her fingers through her hair. "The boy has spent most of his formative years living a very sheltered life, and due to that sheltered upbringing has some rather antiquated views about dating."

"Like?"

"Celibacy."

"Celibacy? As in…?"

"As in saving himself for his wedding night."

"So…that means what?"

"That means I haven't gotten any since I broke up with my ex four months ago."

"Any? At all? Of any kind?"

"Nada. Zip. Zilch."

"So you need?"

Julee leaned in and gave Bobbi a passionate kiss. "I need to feel something."

"Something?"

"Something. Anything. A little. A lot. It doesn't matter at this point what's done or how it's done. I just need to be touched."

Bobbi sat up and gave Julee's breast a gentle squeeze and a light feathering around the areola. Julee bit her bottom lip and slowly stretched herself on top of her bestie. For the next couple of minutes, they both held each other and enjoyed the sensual vibes both were throwing.

"Anything in particular you want to do next?" asked Bobbi, who began running her fingers down Julee's backside.

Biting her lips, she said, "Inside."

"Beg pardon?"

"I haven't gotten anything in the past four months. Not even a hickey….oh man, don't you dare stop that feather touching."

"In case you haven't noticed, I'm not exactly equipped to go inside and do you like a muscle man."

"I know, but I really need to be entered by *something* tonight. I don't care whether it's human or vegetable at this point, I just need to be loved. Boobs."

It was the very rare occasion that Julee would call her by her childhood nickname, because that meant she wanted something very personal from her. Kissing her forehead, she said, "Okay."

Julee sat up and gave Bobbi a deep passionate kiss. She unbuttoned her jeans and rolled them down to her knees. Still kissing Bobbi about the face, she then dipped a finger into her panty waistband and pulled that down as well. Pulling her own down, she then carefully stretched back out and began to gently grind.

This went on for several minutes, with Julee happily grinding away and Bobbi sensually playing her boobs while still feather touching her backside. She eventually worked her fingers down to her ass and began to play with her nether regions as well.

Julee began to stiffer as waves of pleasure began to rock and roll her. Finally, she raised herself up and said in a labored tone, "My Boobi, please pleasure me from the inside! I need your magic fingers now!"

Bobbi looked deep into her friend's eyes and saw both the genuine love and yearning pour out of them. She kissed one of her breasts and carefully inserted two fingers just inside of her nether regions. For the next few minutes, she gently tickled and massaged her friend like they were fast approaching a deadline.

Suddenly Julee straightened out and seized sharply. She grabbed her friend's head, stuffed it between her breasts and left it there until the painful seizures gradually subsided. Eventually, she gave her friend another deep passionate kiss, before carefully rolling off and landing heavily on the carpet.

Julee eventually stood up on wobbly legs and began flexing to get the circulation back. Once done, she sat down on Bobbi's waist and looked deep into her eyes. "I can't tell how much this really means to me, but if you come back later in the day I'll give you a couple of pointers on how you can fix things up with Julias."

Bobbi brushed a few strands of hair from eyes and said, "Will do. I'm glad that you're now feeling better. I better get going 'cause I'm going to need to find a place to crash tonight."

"Oh?"

"Yeah, well, I do share an apartment with Julias and presently, I'm on the outside looking in, if you catch my meaning."

"I see. Well, you can crash here. I can dig out a couple blankets and a pillow---"

"Are you sure? I don't want to be an imposition if you got plans later."

"Boobs, it's three in the morning. The only plans I had was to play video games. Besides, you did me a ginormous favor just now, and the very least I can do is let you crash here for the night. Besides," Julee paused to tweak a nipple. "I can give you a few pointers at breakfast."

Bobbi smiled, and as she watched Julee walk towards the bedroom to retrieve the blankets and pillows, with her tight ass swaying in rhythm, thought about how special and unique their friendship truly was and whispered softly, "I am indeed living the good life."

Red Stripe

"Yo Donnie, where's my makeup kit? I need to get ready for work."

"Right where you left it last time."

Krystal rummaged around the closet for a minute or so, before finding it tucked away on the top shelf between the box of powdered eggnog and the box of dried calamari.

"Got it, thanks."

"Need any help in getting ready?"

"Nah, I'm good to go this time. What time do I have to be at work?"

Donnie looked at his cell phone and said, "Three o'clock."

"Damn."

"What? You got about three hours before you need to be there."

"Three hours ain't gonna cut it. I need at least four. Why didn't you wake me up earlier?"

"Because the smile on your face melted my resolve to get you up in order to make you punctual."

Krystal thought about that smile, and smiled again.

"Yeah. So if you don't need me anymore, I'll let you get ready for work. I'll be back around two thirty to drive you in. Okay?"

"Okay. See ya around two thirty."

Sighing, Krystal walked into the bathroom, turned on the shower, got undressed and hopped in. While she was lathering up and rinsing off, she started going over her checklist for work. By the time she'd finished her shower, she was halfway through the list. Wrapping herself up, she did the rest of her toiletries, and at the same time, finished her checklist.

Walking into the bedroom, she finished squeezing out the water to her waist length hair. Wrapping that up in a turban, she then put on some clean undergarments, before grabbing a brush and the blow dryer, and sitting down on the bed. Undoing the towel, she then spent the next fifteen minutes brushing and blow drying her hair, then the next twenty after that doing her hair into one long simple braid.

When she'd finished, she threw on a black tee-shirt, grabbed her make up kit and sat down in front of the mirror. Taking out a container of white makeup, she applied a liberal amount to her face, creating a ghoulish white base. She then spent the next twenty-five minutes adding various shades of eyeliner, lipstick and other assorted markings about her face.

As a finishing touch, she took out a container of dark cherry red makeup and drew about a half dozen red teardrops running down her left eye.

When she had her face completed to her satisfaction, she then turned her attention to getting dressed. Going from the walk-in closet to a dresser to an old vaudeville traveling trunk, it took her about fifteen minutes to pick out the appropriate clothes she needed to wear. Peeling off her tee-shirt, she checked the condition of her boobs before adding a couple of drops of perfume to her cleavage. Rubbing them together for good luck, in no time at all they were primed, pumped and ready to take out anyone who crossed her path.

She put the black tee-shirt back on, then grabbed a funky pair of knee high horizontal black and white striped socks and a pair of black cutoffs that stopped at mid-thigh. Putting those on, she then grabbed a medium sized chain and a small bicycle lock and wrapped it through the belt loops. Next up was a studded dog collar, which was followed by a pair of silver cross earrings, a Star of David pendant, a black opal nose stud and nail polish: jet black with a small cherry red dot in the center of each nail. The second to the last piece of the ensemble, which she was just starting to lace up when Donnie started honking his horn, were a pair of retro black Converse b-ball sneakers.

Krystal poked her head out of the bedroom window, and said, "Hold on a minute! I'm almost done!"

Donnie looked at his cell and yelled back, "You got about twenty-five minutes before you have to be at work!"

"I know! I have to find my mirrors, then I'll be ready for action! Give me another minute or so!"

"Alright!"

♡

By the time Krystal walked out the door Donnie was already out of the car. Meeting her halfway, he scooped her up and carried her back to the car, where he then stuffed her and the make up kit through the window. Running around to the driver's side, he hopped in and dropped the car into reverse. As he was backing out of the driveway he turned to say something and was met with a right cross to the nose.

Losing control of the car, he accelerated down the driveway and into a speed limit sign. Grabbing his nose, he yelled, "What the fuck was that for?"

"That was for doing what you did to me a few seconds ago. I told you I was going to be right there once I got done getting dressed."

"But we have to make time."

"So what. It's not like they're gonna start without me. I'm the star attraction to this shindig, remember?"

"Well..yeah." Donnie took a look in the rear view mirror at his busted nose. "Christ, I think you broke it. There's blood pouring down my face."

"Let me see."

Krystal grabbed his chin and looked at his nose for a couple of seconds. Snorting, she said, "Please, you're over exaggerating. It's just a small trickle running down your face. Here, take this tissue and switch seats. I'll drive."

"You...drive? My car?"

Donnie suddenly got nervous about Krystal driving. Krystal wasn't one of those so-called *responsible drivers*, since she always managed to accumulate more than her fair share of driving infractions, and right now her d.l. was currently sitting out a ninety day suspension for points over the cap.

"Yes, I'm gonna drive. Don't you worry none, I got a learner's permit."

"A learner's permit? You?"

"Yes, me. Furthermore, it says I have to drive with a responsible adult, and you're the closest thing I got to a responsible adult. Now shut up and let me get going."

Before Donnie could protest further, Krystal had dropped the gearshift and was accelerating down the road.

"Careful with the car! I just bought it a few days ago!"

"You bought this classic Mustang convertible a few days ago and you haven't put it through its paces yet? What kind of man are you anyways?

"One that values his driver's license."

Krystal didn't answer and except for a brief moment when she said yes to him asking if she needed her braid undone, remained silent for the rest of the drive. When she roared into the parking lot, with her waist length jet black hair trailing behind and her ghoulish makeup, she looked liked she stepped straight out of some kind of horror pulpy fiction novel.

Fishtailing into a parking space, Krystal killed the engine and was about to step out when Donnie grabbed her arm. Pulling her arm away, she turned and gave him a dirty look. He placed his hand on her neck and began massaging. A minute or so into it, he thought he saw a brief look of contentment pass over her face, before it resumed its current mask of irritability.

Concerned, he leaned over and whispered, "I'm sorry."

Relaxing a bit, she stroked his thigh and said, "I know you are. That's what I love most about you." Touching his cheek, she added, "We made good time today, so I got a couple of spare minutes to play with."

"You'll ruin your makeup."

"I'll take that chance."

She gave him a heartfelt kiss, which he returned the same way. Getting out, she walked over to his side and waited for him to finish lowering the seat. Climbing in, she stretched out on top of him, and they promptly spent the next couple of minutes making out like a couple of love struck teenagers. When she finally disengaged, she rested her head on his muscular chest and closed her eyes. Not wanting to interrupt the moment, Donnie carefully took out the compact from Krystal's back pocket and gently pinched her thigh.

"What?" she said rather soberly, as she didn't really want this quiet moment to end just yet.

Donnie opened the compact and said, "Your makeup needs to be readjusted."

Krystal turned head and saw that Donnie was indeed correct about her makeup. Sighing hard, she peeled herself off and sat up. Sitting cross-legged on his lap, she had him hold the compact while she took out her make up kit and touched up her face. Giving the mirror an air kiss, she put her make up kit on the on the windshield and climbed out of the car.

Limbering up for a few seconds, she shook her hair out and asked, "Hey sweets, can you grab that small bottle of glitter and spray a little bit into my hair?"

Donnie sat up and asked, "Where?"

"Under the front seat."

"How?"

"Don't ask. Can you do it for me or not?"

"Sure."

Donnie grabbed the bottle and got out of the car. Shaking it briefly, he then gave her hair a half dozen spritzs, fluffed it, then gave it another half dozen. When he'd finished, he asked, "How's that?"

"How would I know? I'm not exactly surrounded by mirrors ya know. Do I look okay?"

"Twirl."

Krystal twirled, and Donnie confirmed his original assessment.

"Great." She stepped forward and gave him a small peck on the nose. "I'll see you later in the evening. Don't worry about picking me up, I'll grab a taxi. Have fun and try not to worry."

As she walked towards the entrance, Donnie yelled, "Can't help it, I love you too much."

Krystal gave him a hair flip and ran to catch up with her sister-in-law Minnie. Donnie waited until she entered the building, before hopping into the car to drive away. As he was leaving the parking lot, his cell phone rang. Taking it out, he saw a text from Krystal. It said, "You know, I really do love you.

Please worry about me, as it helps keep me grounded for the night. TTYL."

Donnie smiled and accelerated out of the parking lot.

Krystal handed her cell to Minnie before putting on her mirrors and a surgical mask. Fluffing her hair one last time, she said to Minnie, "Okay babe, I'm as ready as I'm ever gonna be. It's show time!"

Minnie smiled and grabbed the mike from one of the enforcers. On her way to the stage, she started playing to the audience, high fiving and egging them on. By the time she stepped onto the stage, the crowd was white hot and ready to explode in a testosterone/estrogen fueled rage. Doing one last ceiling pump, Minnie roared into the microphone like a tiger in heat.

"Ladies and gentlemen, boys and girls, adults of ages! Hellion's is proud to present to you, the act that has come back from a very successful penitentiary tour of the east coast, the one, the only, Krystal Methadone!!!!

Krystal hits the stage like a woman possessed and starts off the show by sledgehammering the audience with an intricate speed metal version of "I'm Down". When last note fades, the band shifted gears into overdrive and ripped through two dozen sub-three minute punk/speed metal instrumentals, with Krystal growling, moaning, twitching and writhing all over the stage.

By the time the last note fades, Krystal has the audience totally twisted around her little finger. She takes a seat on the edge of the stage and waits for the band to wind down. Once they do, she sends them off on a much needed fifteen minute break. Before they leave, the lead guitarist throws an acoustic guitar to her, so that she can do the second set.

Donnie first met Krystal about a year and a half ago when they were each taking the same music theory class at the local community college. At the time, she was a classical guitar player and he was a local folk singer. They got to talking during the class, and one night he invited her to perform with him at an open mike night sponsored by the local coffeehouse.

She accepted and their performance was such a rousing success that they were invited back for a semi-regular gig. Eventually those performances and their partnership led to a more intimate relationship and six months later, they were sharing a house, and four months after that, they were married.

One night, Donnie met up with some friends at a local club called Hellion's. They were going on about a hot new punk/speed metal band. It featured a rather lithe girl who was dressed from head to toe in black and wearing KISS style makeup with her hair glittered out, and their stage show was something straight out of an Alice Cooper/Insane Clown Posse concert.

When they hit the stage and began playing, the music simply blew Donnie away. The combination of the punk and speed metal worked him over with a jackhammer efficiency that left him gasping for air. By the time the first set ended, he was ready to call it quits. But then he saw the lead singer sit on the edge of the stage, which gave him the opportunity to one, get a better look and two, find out a little bit about her.

Once he got closer though, he saw much to his surprise, that it was his lovely wife Krystal who was performing for the S.R.O. crowd. Intrigued about this unknown facet of his wife, Donnie hung around for the rest of the show plus the encore. Afterwards, he left with the rest of his friends and headed for home.

Some two hours later, his wife walked in looking like something the cat dragged in. Donnie asked her how was work, she answered that it was a very long night. He responded by saying that he kind of figured that, because he happened to catch her show at the club. Shocked that he found out about her secret life, Crystal dropped to the couch and began crying her eyes out.

Donnie waited a few seconds, before taking a seat next to her. Gently cradling her in his arms, they spent the rest of the night talking about her second career, their marriage and how to run and meld both parts for the future. When morning arrived, Donnie became the manager and personal assistant for the punk/speed metal band Krystal Methadone.

Because of the type of music that Krystal Methadone played and the type of clubs they were playing at, Donnie had legitimate reasons for becoming Mylanta's best customer. After several months of non-stop touring, they had finally hit that level of pain that all punk/metal bands strive for: rioting. They'd become so popular that their concerts were attracting the darker side of their chosen genre: the disaffected and the disenfranchised. Those unnatural elements, combined with the home grown that were already involved, created a powder keg of epic proportions.

Violence became the rule instead of the exception, as moshing and slamming became semi-permanent fixtures at their concerts. Fighting was soon added to the unholy duo of drinking and drugging, and soon after one concert in which scores of people were injured (along with one fatality), private security became part and parcel to all performances.

In addition to private security being added, other changes were made. The mini-mosh pits were closed, and new concert times were created. No longer were concerts starting at ten and lasting until the wee hours of the morning; instead, they were now starting no later than three and finishing in the early evening. Finally, a much needed music swerve in the form of Krystal's first love, the classical guitar, was installed.

Most of these adjustments worked to perfection. They were first introduced during the band's east cost penitentiary tour and while there were some tense moments during a few of the concerts, overall that tour was a rousing success. Even though Donnie was able to cut down on his Mylanta intake, the true test was going to be whether or not those adjustments were going to work tonight.

Most of the changes were already being done at the various clubs, but the one that was starting to cause the severest amount of personal stress, was the music swerve. It was one ting to change between punk and speed metal, but to change from something that was filled with smoldering rage to something that was filled with passion, could backfire in ways that would make the evening news.

Donnie was trying not to be the worrier that Krystal gently mocked him for, but was failing miserably. No matter what he did to keep himself occupied, black thoughts of violent retribution kept creeping back in and kept him reaching for the Mylanta.

Stepping outside for some fresh air, he heard his cell phone go off. Thinking the worse, he took one last swig of Mylanta, before reluctantly answering the phone. Flipping the cover, he saw the phrase, *Incoming Text from Minnie*. Pushing a couple of buttons, he brought the message up, which read, "2nd set engaged."

He responded, "keep in touch."

Sighing, he put the phone away, took a seat on the porch, and soon became lost within the confines of his mind.

"Wooooo!!! How ya'll doing to*night?* I want ta thank you for being here, at Hellion's!!!! Tonight we're gonna be doing something just a little bit different." <strums the guitar for a couple of seconds> "The band went off for a short break to refresh and recharge their batteries and for the next twenty minutes, I'm gonna be giving you a taste," <sticks out her chest and jiggles it for a few seconds> "of something passionate, something sensual, and something just a liiiiiittle bit naughty."

Krystal jiggled her chest again, and a low roar fills the air. She then bends all the way back until she's horizontal, all the while shaking them for maximum effective. Stretching out, she quickly rips off her tee-shirt, and jumps up to show off her attributes that are barely held in by her diamond studded lace bra.

Flipping her hair, she moves towards a nearby microphone stand and stool. Sitting down, she says only one word, "Delgadina."

The audience becomes spellbound as Krystal plays an intricate story song about an incestuous relationship in Medieval Spain. The ones closest to the stage watch in jaw dropping amazement as the fingers on her right hand move gracefully up and down the frets, while the fingers on her left fly like the wind as they pluck strings to create a vivid picture of nineteenth century Spain.

Just as abruptly as the song started, so it ends in the same fashion. Krystal briefly stretches out and shakes her head for a moment. She looks up, gives an evil smile, then drops a cup of ice cubes into her cleavage. Shuddering, she says, "Recuedros de la Alhambra." then whips right into the sensual gypsy dance song.

Right away, a low murmur of displeasure erupts from the audience, as they become restless from listening to yet another acoustic rambling of the hottest punk babe on the planet. Krystal looks up from her playing and catches the bad vibes from the audience head on. Worried, she nevertheless continues playing, but flips her hair a couple of times and briefly looks offstage.

Thirty seconds later, the lead guitarist strolls onstage and heads towards Krystal. He starts tapping his heel so as to pick up her playing rhythm, then in smooth motion, replaces her hand on the frets with his. Krystal maintains the same pace, but starts to get down off the stool. The guitarist reaches around and on a silent three count, takes the place of Krystal on the guitar.

Dripping with sweat, Krystal pauses for a minute to catch her breath and to pick up the rhythm of the song again. Carefully moving her hair from face, she then moves the microphone away from the stool. Again giving an evil smile, she wraps herself around the microphone like she's making love to it and starts to accompany the guitarist in Spanish.

Between the lyrical complexity of the song and the sensual body movements, the previous murmurs of displeasure were soon replaced by a testosterone/estrogen fueled sexual awakening among the audience. Once again, Krystal had the upper hand and worked it to maximum perfection.

As she got deeper into the song, the passion that was behind the lyrics poured out of her like a non-stop climax. She hugged the microphone like a lover and caressed the stand like it was the hottest thing on stage. Untwisting the holder, she followed the slow drop like she was impaling herself on her lover's rod. By the time she got to the ground, she was straddling the microphone like it was the only thing left on the planet that could satisfy her personal ache.

As the final bars where being played, Krystal slowly leaned back until her forehead was touching the stage. As the last note was being played, she slowly flattened out, brought her hair forward and covered herself with it like a blanket.

The stage soon after went dark. Noise could be heard from both the audience, who were now voicing their approval of her performance, and from the rest of the band who had finished their break and were heading back to the stage. While the band was getting itself situated, Krystal had taken off her bra and stuck four pieces of tape on her nipples.

On a silent count of three, the stage exploded in a mini pyrotechnic display as the band opened up the second half of the concert with their cover of Motorhead's "Ace of Spades". Krystal jumps up and with hair flying all over, immediately added her unique vocals to the mix. Ratcheting up the tempo, in no time at all, the testosterone completely destroyed everything else as moshing made its violent return to Hellion's.

Minnie was taking all of this in with a mixture of shock and awe. Once again, Krystal Methadone had the crowd twisted so tightly around their collective fingers that there was no telling what would happen if the rubber band popped; and shock with what Krystal had done in order to work the crowd into such a feverish pitch. Her main concern now was making sure that the concert didn't get halted due to what Krystal wasn't wearing. At this point, Minnie saw that Krystal was basically dressed like the legendary Wendy O. Williams, in that she was wearing electrical tape across her nipples, her panties, and her socks and sneakers. And the panties were starting to drop as Krystal's movements got more violent and exaggerated. Still, her makeup was pretty much intact as she made doubly sure not to wipe the sweat from her brow.

Minnie stepped outside for a few minutes so that she could get some much needed fresh air, and to also let Donnie know what her opinion was on the second set. Dialing him up, she waited for the phone to connect. While she was waiting, she called the bouncer over and said, "Keep an eye on the stage, because if anything freaky starts to happen, the show will be shut down. Understand?"

Minnie didn't wait for a response as Donnie suddenly came on the line.

"How'd it go?" he asked.

"Sensational. Although—"

"No."

"But you don't even know what I was going to say."

"Yeah, I do," he said in a tone that he'd hoped would cut off further discussion.

When the band decided to tweak their stage show, one of the things discussed was what Krystal just did. Donnie was against it for a couple of reasons: one, the potential for Krystal to get carried away with the sexual explicitness of her performance and thus getting arrested; and two, the potential for rioting. The band argued for it because of the potential for rioting if the crowds were forced to listen to straight classical guitar. Donnie eventually agreed to a test run in the smaller venues, and so far all of the concerts went off without a hitch. Tonight's at Hellion's was the starting point for the larger venues. Depending on what happened there would determine how the rest of the shows would be planned.

Minnie understood where Donnie was coming from, simply because she knew her brother better than he knew himself sometimes. "I suppose you do at that, which would explain why you aren't here, right?"

"Right." Donnie paused for a moment as he tried to remember what it was he wanted to ask.

Minnie sensed there was something else that Donnie wanted to ask. "Was there something else you wanted to ask, because I need to get back inside."

"Yeah. How's she looking?"

"Hot."

"Figuratively?"

"As always."

Before Donnie could respond, he heard a loud roar in the background, just before Minnie's phone went dead. Fearing the worst, he stuffed his phone into his jeans and jumped in the car. Accelerating out of the driveway, he quickly shifted gears and burned rubber to the club.

The roar that Donnie heard was the beginning of a full scale riot at the club. One of the bouncers came staggering out with blood pouring down his face, and collapsed in Minnie's arms. Just before he passed out, he was able to tell her that someone made a grab for Krystal, and that Krystal responded by kicking the guy in the face. All hell broke loose as the guys friends jumped in and the band jumped in as well. Minnie left the bouncer with a passerby, who she told to dial 911 and headed back inside.

Inside was chaos and pandemonium as everyone had chosen sides and was beating the shit out of each other with whatever they were able to get their hands on. Minnie grabbed a broken pool cue and started slashing and hacking her way to the stage. When she got there, she saw that Krystal was lying in someone's lap with a knife sticking out of her stomach. Climbing up, she ran over and watched in horror as the drummer closed her eyes and brought her hair forward.

Minnie screamed and dropped to her knees. Picking up Krystal, she jerkily ran her hands over her lifeless body. Brushing her hair aside, she brought her closer and began crying hysterically. It took four people to carefully pull her away from Krystal. Babbling incoherently, Minnie was gently scooped up by the drummer and carried outside.

Donnie had blown into the parking lot and as soon as he got close enough to the building he jumped out and ran to the entrance. He got there just as a bloodied and battered Minnie was being carried out. He gave the drummer a questioning look, who returned it with a tearful throw of his head towards the gurney that was being wheeled out. Before anyone could stop him, he ran over and pulled off the bloodstained sheet.

There laying before him, looking remarkably serene, was Krystal. He stared at her face for a full minute, before saying, "Wait a minute."

He grabbed a washcloth from a nearby paramedic and spent the next couple of minutes taking off her makeup. When he'd finished, he caressed her cheek for a few seconds then gave her a brief but passionate kiss, before turning away in tears.

After the ambulance left, Donnie walked over to the drummer and took possession of Minnie. With tears running down his face, he took a seat on the curb and cradling Minnie in his lap, Donnie spent the rest of the night crying his eyes out and thinking about the star that went supernova much too soon.

The Inner Sibling

PROLOGUE: SUNDAY

"I need an extension."

"I've already given you two, Jeannie."

"Please, Uncle Rudy, I'm asking you as a close family member. You know what I've been going through for the past couple of months."

He didn't answer straight off, probably giving that particular fact thought for several seconds. Then he gave an exasperated sigh. "Okay. Because you've been the only one in the family who still speaks to me on a regular basis, in spite of what I do for a living, I'll give you until Friday evening to get me the money. That's five days from now. Otherwise, I take what they want. Understand?"

"Perfectly. Thanks a lot, Uncle Rudy. This really means a lot to me. I won't let you down."

"You better not, because I'd really hate to do to you what I do to everyone else."

Jeannie went cold and gulped hard. "I promise."

"That's my niece. I'll talk to you on Friday, at my usual place. Take care."

"You too."

Jeannie hung up the phone and thought about what a mess her life had become. Her company had downsized her about a year and a half ago, and between the unemployment compensation and the severance pay, she was just barely making ends meet. With no permanent job prospects on the horizon, she'd lost her lazy boyfriend; he'd decided to break with her when she told him he had to start paying his own way. Money had gotten so scarce that she was forced to take out a loan on her motorcycle. Since her credit wasn't very good, she had to use an acquaintance of her uncle's to secure the monies.

He really didn't want to do it, because he had a lot of respect for her and Rudy -- but by using her natural assets, she was able to wear down his resistance to the point of getting not only the loan but getting it on her terms. Initially she made her payments on time, due to being able to supplement her dwindling funds with the occasional temp job, but that fell by the wayside and soon thereafter she became tardy with her payments.

The tardiness finally got to be so bad that her Uncle Rudy had to step in and deliver an ultimatum: money by Friday or face the consequences. She shuddered at the prospect of what would happen if he was forced to do to her what he normally did everyone else who was late with their payments. Still, she appreciated the fact that he thought enough of her to give her a five-day window to get current with her payments. What bothered her now was how she was going to raise two thousand dollars by Friday evening.

Sighing, she pulled out the afternoon paper and stretched out on the park bench. As she was perusing the want ads, taking notes and circling potential job opportunities, somebody sat down one bench over from her and began whistling a lively tune. Intrigued, she looked up to see who was whistling and was surprised to find a rather doughy-looking young man tipping his baseball cap to her.

"Hi there."

"Hi yourself," said Jeannie as she sat up and put aside her newspaper.

"Great day to be out at the park, isn't it?"

"Not if you got a problem like I do."

"Oh? Sorry to hear that. Anything I can do to help?"

"Not unless you know where I can come up with two thousand dollars by Friday."

"Ouch! Two k is a serious chunk of change. …However, I may be able to help."

"Really?"

"Really. By the way, my name is Ken."

"Jeannie. So what kind of help could you possibly give me?"

"Well, for starters, here's my card." Ken pulled out a small blue and yellow business card and handed it to Jeannie.

Jeannie took it and read the contents. "Ken Epee, Line 21 Productions. So, Ken Epee of Line 21 Productions, what is it that you do?"

"I help good looking men and women use the vast potential of their beings to earn the maximum amount of money that they're entitled to."

"Come again?"

"Exactly."

Jeannie thought about Ken's last comment for a moment, then went wide eyed. "Not on your life! I'm not that desperate! I have morals, you know." She handed the card back to Ken.

Ken held up his hand and said, "Of course you do. But sometimes we can reach a point in our lives where we ask ourselves, 'Am I doing the very best for myself and my family? What can I do to stave off the bill collectors, foreclosure, bankruptcy, welfare?' If you've got the attributes, why not use them to your advantage?"

Jeanie scrunched up her face and said, "I don't know. This just doesn't sound right. It sounds…."

"Dirty? Of course it is. But if you approach it like a business, then you can rise above the dirtiness and make a good living at it. Look, there are plenty of other jobs in the adult entertainment industry: pole-dancing, lap dancing, exotic dancing, and even stripping. The movie industry is just another segment that can specialize – safely – in whatever turns people on. You'd be amazed at what people do to get their rocks off. Why not take full advantage of it? Besides, you said yourself that you need to come up with two K by Friday, and I'm assuming that if you don't, something bad will happen. Right?"

Jeannie shuddered, and said, "Something very bad."

"Well alright then. Look," Ken took the card and scribbled an address on the back of it. "Be at this address tomorrow by nine sharp, and I promise that we'll find something for you that will maximize what you've got -- and just at first glance, you've got a lot to maximize. Besides, what have you got to lose?"

"My self-respect."

"No, you'll always have that. Remember what I said; if you treat it like a business, then you can rise above the dirt. Don't let it own you; you own it, and by owning it, you'll always have that self-respect. Nobody can take that from you. Nobody."

Jeannie watched as Ken took out his cell-phone to take a call. Giving her a quick four finger wave, he got up and walked towards the park entrance. In a matter of minutes, he disappeared from sight. Sighing, she lifted the card and read the address on the back, before sticking it in her jeans and turning her attention back to the help-wanted ads.

Jeannie spent the next couple of hours reading, but not comprehending, the ads. Every time she tried to take notes or make phone calls, her mind kept going back to the business card that Ken had left behind. Every time she got distracted by that card, she would take it out and study it for a couple of minutes, before returning it to her pocket. The distraction soon got to be so bad that she finally packed up her newspaper and went home.

Even at home the card was still a distraction, because every time she got to thinking about her current situation, her mind kept wandering back to that card. Finally, six hours after Ken had left his card, Jeannie decided to have a long talk with Aissa.

The first thing she did was to make sure that the front door was locked. On her way to the bedroom, she grabbed a chair from the kitchen and placed it in front of the full length wall mirror. She then went to the window and closed the curtains, and was about to take a seat in the chair when her symbiont Aissa appeared in the mirror and started giving her what-for over the prospect of doing adult movies.

"So, you think you got what it takes to do adult movies?" asked Aissa.

"Yes. I believe I do have what it takes to do adult movies. After all, I've got the looks and—"

"Doesn't mean a thing, sweetie. You can't even wear something like a tight T-shirt, because -- heaven forbid -- someone might compliment you on your natural assets.'

"Excuse me? I'll have you know that I've worn tight T-shirts before."

"In your apartment doesn't count. It's out there that counts, and if you're gonna do adult movies, you'll really have to flaunt everything."

"So how hard can that be? I can flaunt them just as well as anybody else."

"'How hard can that be'? I can't believe you just said that! You can't even get nude in the daytime unless you're getting ready to take a shower, and as for sex -- pfft."

"That's a lie, and you know it."

"Okay. Prove me wrong – take off your shirt and bra."

"What?"

"You heard me. Take off your shirt and bra. Better yet, strip completely -- so we can get a good look at that fantastic bod of yours."

Jeannie hesitated for a moment, but that hesitation was all that Aissa needed to prove her point. "Loser. I am so out of here."

"Oh yeah? I don't recall asking your permission to do what I see fit with this body of mine! If doing adult movies gets me the money that I need, in order to not wind up like one my uncle's deadbeats, then so be it. Furthermore, I'm gonna prove just how wrong you are about me being ashamed of flaunting it."

Jeannie grabbed the chair and flung it out of the bedroom. Giving the mirror a couple of hard taps to get Aissa's attention, she took a few steps back and sat on the bed. She then untied her sneakers, and threw each one at the mirror. Lying down, she sucked in her stomach and unbuttoned her cutoffs and started to take them off, but then changed her mind and simply kept them on.

Sitting back up, she untied her blouse and, after taking it off, threw that at the mirror. By the time she was ready to take off her midriff, Aissa had decided to reappear.

"About time you showed back up. So I'm afraid to flaunt it, eh? Well, take a look at these ebony pearls."

Sticking a couple of fingers under the band, she quickly pulled off her midriff and showed Aissa what had to be the shapeliest ebony pearls that anyone had ever seen. She tapped them a couple of times so as to air them out, blew the mirror a kiss, and walked out of the bedroom to spend the rest of the evening getting used to parading around topless without freaking out.

She first went into the kitchen to grab some leftover Chinese from the fridge, and when she opened the door the blast of refrigerated air gave her body a major shock as goosebumps instantly appeared on her arms and chest. Shivering, she grabbed the leftovers and a bottle of beer and walked over to the living room. She turned on the big oscillating fan, she then sat down on the couch, grabbed the remote and spent the rest of the evening pigging out on leftovers, chilling out to the sensual stylings of 70's Chicago Soul, and finally falling asleep on the couch.

Around midnight, Aissa poked her head into Jeannie's mind to see how she was handling being topless. After observing her latest dream for a few seconds, and turning a deep shade of red, she quietly stepped all the way in and took control of Jeannie's body so that she could get her to bed.

After a couple of false starts, in which Aissa kept falling back onto the couch because she couldn't quite coordinate the legs properly, she finally was able to establish a good rhythm and within a minute got Jeannie in the bedroom. It took another minute to get her tucked in, and when she felt that Jeannie was back in a regular breathing rhythm, she quietly stepped out, gave her a kiss on the cheek and disappeared back into her world.

Other Books by G.B. Miller

All of my published works, both in print and e-book can be found on Amazon.

My profile:
www.amazon.com/G.B.-Miller/e/B00B3XMZ2O

Connect with G.B. Miller

You can follow me on Facebook:
www.facebook.com/booksbygbmjrofct

You can follow me on Blogger:
ctsgbmjr2019.blogspot.com

www.ingramcontent.com/pod-product-compliance
Lightning Source LLC
Chambersburg PA
CBHW020643160726
47991CB00003B/1006